# The Adventures of
# Enu

By Sebastian Slovin

Illustrated by Blaze Syka

Edited by Donn "Bernie" Bernstein

*The Adventures of Enu: The Tale of the Giant Whale*
Published November 2012
By Sebastian Slovin
Solana Beach, CA

Layout and Design by Blaze Syka and Sebastian Slovin

*Thank you Mom and Tanasa for never giving up.*

Forward,

It is with great enthusiasm and gratitude that I have the opportunity to introduce you to Enu. The legend was passed down to me from my father. When I was very young he would tell me adventurous tales of this mystical creature from all over the world. Now it is my turn to share Enu with you. This is Enu's debut into the public forum - a literary lair to preserve his lore. Since I first heard about Enu my life has never been the same. Enu has changed the way I see the world and it is my hope that he does the same for you.

Such is the legend of Enu - part human, part mammal, part plant and a blend of components beyond - who could as likely evolve, and appear, from elm to elephant or from hawk to hummingbird. He could be an eagle from the heavens he guarded, a monkey from the jungles he inhabited, a lizard from the creek beds where he slept or a goat from the mountains he climbed. Enu has soared with the condors, engaged the elks, crawled with armies of ants, slithered with snakes, dove with dolphins and gravitated to the great whites.

Enu is a symbol of synergy and congeniality, a lovable and refreshing figure of trust and faith and a committed crusader for global unification. His affection for youth is palpable and his determination to bridge all barriers of the world is noble and noteworthy. I hope you enjoy the Legend of Enu.

Sebastian Slovin
Solana Beach, California, September 2012

It was early morning and the winds were swirling as a tiny hummingbird sat perched on the power line above the white house. The house was one of several similar structures sprawled throughout a vast neighborhood. The wind blew strong on this early summer day, sweeping the clouds quickly across a threatening sky, casting shadows over the rows of residences below. There was something special about this day. Perhaps it was the whirl of the wind or the birds serenading the neighborhood with their distinctive tweeting, squawking and singing with unusual excitement. Perched high in the trees - on chimney tops, telephone poles and street lamps - their echoes drifted from sky high to the bushes below. The hummingbird who graced the power line was singing, too. Its song, mixed with the chirping chorus of the other birds, blended with the whistle of the swirling wind, creating a beautiful sound if anyone was around to hear it.

Inside the white house, below the singing hummingbird, the feeling was quite different. The rooms and hallways were strangely empty, devoid of delightful song. There sat the boy, alone, a restless youth slumped and staring at the blaring television. He sat and flipped mindlessly from channel to channel, but no images captured his attention or imagination. Summer vacation had just begun for the boy, who was already bored rather than buoyed by a trip to his beloved beach.

One month earlier, when the family uprooted from the only house he had known as home, the boy emerged lost and languishing in an unfamiliar home in foreign territory.

The family had relocated from a beautiful lively coastal town to a quiet inland suburb. The youngster found himself stranded in the middle of nowhere. Painfully robbed of the pleasures of his favorite pastime - riding the waves on his cherished surfboard with friends in tow - the adventure seeker felt lost in loneliness. Here he was, on summer vacation and stranded in a boring house in a boring neighborhood with nothing to do but brood. To the boy it couldn't get much worse than this.

He just sat there, bored, frustrated and thinking about all the fun he would be having if only he could go surfing! Even his diverted glances out the living room window left him defeated while watching reruns on television.

*Nothing exciting could possibly happen in this neighborhood*, thought the lad, who was lost in the doldrums of despair.

There were the same boring trees in the backyard, the same drab houses beyond that, the same clouds, and the same sky, just as it had been every day since moving to this no man's land. The boy looked out the window again and noticed that the wind seemed to be much stronger than normal on this morning. He watched as it whipped through the trees in the backyard, causing branches to flutter in fury.  As he continued to stare blankly, the boy heard a loud bang and the television shut off with a SNAP! The power was out!

His eyes searched the spacious room. It was dark and uncomfortably quiet.

*Could this summer possibly get any worse?* the youth wondered.

As he looked back out the living room window, the boy sensed something intriguing about the wind on this jittery June day. He had not been outside much since moving to the white house and while he considered going out, he didn't know where to go or what to do.  He sat on the couch for a little while longer but the eerie silence was stifling. The boy rubbed his eyes and then stood up, grabbed his jacket, and headed out the door.

He walked slowly along the sidewalk, shoulders slouched and head down. The birds were still singing all about, but the boy paid them no attention.

"Man, I wish I could surf! There is nothing to do in this boring neighborhood," he complained aloud to no one in particular.

He made his way along the sidewalk beneath the trees, kicking at the dried leaves as they swirled around his feet. As the boy continued to walk he came to what looked to be the entrance of a park he had not previously seen. The boy stopped at the entry, his eyes darting in all directions. Unlike the hustle and bustle of his hometown where locals gathered at the parks

and beaches, here there was no one in sight. Aroused by curiosity, he decided to enter the park and made his way across a small cobblestone bridge that passed over a beautiful duck pond. He quietly walked over to the grassy bank of the blue-green pond, where he sat down on the gentle slope under the tall trees.

The birds in the park were scurrying in an absolute frenzy. The wind was swirling, blowing leaves from the trees and sending ripples across the normally calm pond. The ducks were quacking as they chased each other in playful pursuit while the sparrows and finches darted and fluttered through the air. The woodpeckers were pecking, and the crows were crowing! But the boy didn't notice. He was consumed with thinking about where he would rather be.

A few minutes had passed and he was just about to give up on the boring park when suddenly a hummingbird zoomed down from above and hovered mere inches in front of the youngster's face! The loud buzzing noise from its rapidly beating wings completely startled the boy, who didn't move a muscle but just sat there stunned into silence. He stared at the tiny bird, which was now hovering perfectly in place, and oddly enough seemed to be staring back at the boy.

Mesmerized by the scene, the boy could feel a strong humming within his own chest.  He had never seen a hummingbird so close and was amazed at the exquisite details of its beauty. The boy, now wide-eyed, noticed something peculiar about the markings on this particular bird. It had a narrow streak of white feathers beginning between its eyes and broadened as it went back over its tiny head. The boy jumped back as the hummingbird suddenly made a very high sharp series of chirps, as if trying to awaken him.

As the bird called out, it flashed a brilliant patch of ruby red feathers on its throat. The hummingbird then slowly hovered straight up high into the sky, making another profound call before zooming over the trees, flying deeper into the park. The boy sat and watched with amazement as the tiny bird disappeared into the distance.

The bewildered lad looked around to see if there was anyone who saw what had just happened.

*What was that all about?* he thought.

Maybe there was more to this park than there seemed. A smile creased the boy's lips for the first time since he moved from the beach. He then stretched out on the soft blanket of grass and stared into the heavens. He looked up through the trees and watched the clouds moving across the sky. A strong gust of wind suddenly whipped the tree branches as leaves scattered about the inquisitive visitor and ominous clouds quickly began to gather and darken overhead. The boy felt a chill as a cold shadow was cast over the park, and a tiny raindrop fell on his shoulder, followed by a few more. The droplets multiplied until the rain fell steadily, dampening his spirit as well as drenching the park. The boy cursed his luck and then stood up to search for some shelter. He looked across the park and in the distance he spotted a grove of imposing trees that promised ample cover from the rain.

His world appeared dark and gloomy as he forged his way through the rain-soaked depths of the park.  Trudging forth, he observed how the trees were increasingly becoming more dense.  He then paused at a small clearing in the forest, looking upward in awe upon confronting a goliath of a tree. It was twice the size of its neighbors, with resounding roots rising out of the soil which turned into a massive trunk standing tall and wide. Huge limbs split off from the trunk, twisting and turning in all directions, supporting a giant canopy of leaves which offered nearly complete cover from the rain. The boy ambled over and sat huddled beneath this towering shelter, yet he was not totally protected as an occasional drop of water fell on his head and shoulders.  Finding refuge, the explorer sat curled up with his head down and his arms folded tightly, hoping for the rain to stop so he could exit the park without getting doused.

Suddenly, a voice called out with excitement from high above, "Isn't this amazing?"

Startled, the boy quickly jumped to his feet and looked up. He stepped back and searched the tree but couldn't see anyone. Again, that strange voice called out, "Isn't it amazing? What a perfect time to see it!"

The boy continued to look up the tree in search of life, but none was to be found. Now frightened, he yelled out, "Who's there?"

Then he spotted it. Towards the top of the towering sentinel there perched a strange little orange animal sitting on a branch looking down at the boy. He watched in amazed curiosity as the unique creature quickly and nimbly climbed down from atop the tree. To be sure, this was the most bizarre adventure the lad had ever encountered!  There in front of him stood an unidentifiable critter that was all of two feet tall and looked like a funny little orange-colored monkey standing on its hind legs. The boy had no idea what this 'thing' was - a miracle or a mirage? The little creature had two arms, two legs, and a long tail. It had huge owl-sized eyes and funny little ears that poked out to the side. It was bright orange in color, whose fluorescence stood out against the darkness of this rainy, dreary day.  This unknown entity also had a streak of white fur on its face, which started narrow between its huge eyes and broadened as it went back over its head, much like the hummingbird the boy had previously encountered.

He jumped back with fright as the little animal said in perfect English, "Come with me! What are you waiting for?  There's no time to waste, it's a beautiful day!"

Still in shock the boy said nothing, standing frozen in time.

The little animal smiled, looked up at this petrified person, and said, "Sorry, I forgot to introduce myself. I am Enu."

The boy thought he was dreaming, unable to separate reality from fantasy.

"I'm sorry if I scared you back there but I wanted to attract your attention.  I didn't mean to fly so close to you. You see I haven't flown in a little while and it always takes me a bit to warm up," Enu confided.

Totally astonished, the boy managed to say, "Wait. What?  What do you mean? That was you back there? You can talk? What are you?"

"I will explain everything later," replied Enu. "Come with me, we don't have much time!" Enu walked out from under the cover of the huge tree and into the rain.

The boy searched the park again to see if anyone else was there to witness this crazy little character, but there was no one in sight. He saw an incredible opportunity to hang out with a talking orange monkey-like animal, so he followed Enu's call. It was clear to the boy that Enu genuinely enjoyed the rain and he apprehensively followed the little animal as it walked deeper into the park before stopping at a juncture where the grass gave way to the start of a hiking trail.

Enu turned around and enthusiastically said, "Quick! Take off your shoes!"

"What? But it's raining," replied the befuddled lad. "Exactly!" said Enu.

The boy found this to be a curious request, but took off his shoes to be polite. He found the carpet of wet soil to be comforting as he followed Enu along the trail, stimulated by each step in the cool mud and the little pebbles and prickly grass.

Enu turned back again and said, "Take care when you walk."
"What do you mean?" asked the eager explorer.
"Look!" said Enu, pointing to the ground.

The boy paused in the rain and looked down at his bare feet on the wet earth. The ground suddenly seemed intensely alive. He stood there in wonder, realizing there was something living beneath his feet.

Enu smiled and said, "You're beginning to see it!"

The boy knelt down to get a closer look, and placed his hands gently on the slippery surface of the soaked soil. It appeared that he was standing on top of and touching the back of an enormous creature that surely was alive. It looked like the tough shiny skin of a colossal animal. It seemed as if the youngster was standing on the back of a giant whale!

*Take care when you walk*, thought the boy, as he stood up and continued slowly along the trail, cautious of each step.

He noticed that everything around him took on a different view. The trunks of the trees, now glistening after a shiny coat of rain, began to look curiously alive, too, like limbs of a grand animal. Nothing seemed to be separate from anything else. He suddenly saw the trees and the plants and the rocks and all within his vision - even himself - as an extension of one extraordinary living being. The boy began to experience not only his environment - but the world - as he never had before.

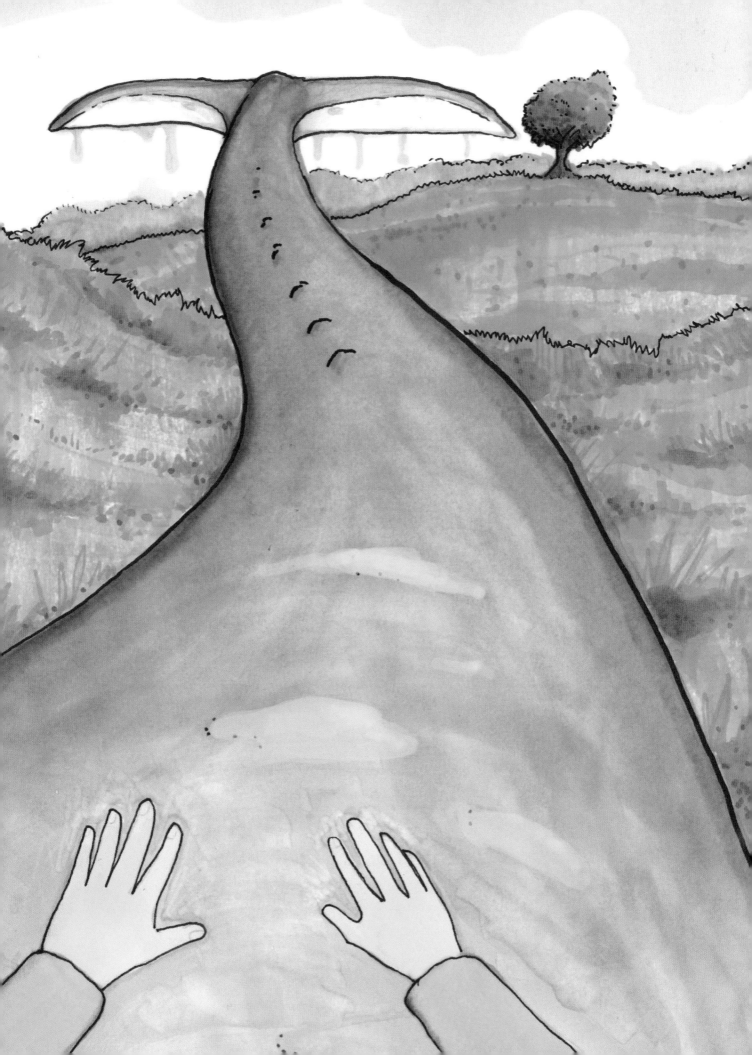

His sensory system, all of a sudden, became appreciably sharpened. His remarkable transition included a renewed sense of smell for strong scents of sage and eucalyptus, as well as a refreshing, brighter and clearer vision for the entire spectrum of color. The boy even began to hear and appreciate the songs of birds he had never heard. Their chips and chirps bounced off the surrounding bushes and trees creating beautiful music enhanced by a gentle wind rustling through the leaves. As the rain was easing and the clouds parting, the lad lavished in a landscape filled with the vivid richness of heart and soul.

Enu turned to the boy and said, "Yes, now you see!"

The boy smiled as they continued this joyous journey along the path to passion and purpose. This was a whole new world for the wide-eyed wonderer.

The boy watched the enchanting little Enu, who was completely fascinated and absorbed in every aspect of nature. Beyond that, Enu was communicating with a wide variety of plants and animals as they walked along the park's inviting paths. Enu would crouch down to watch an ant cross the trail, and then stand up to wave at birds flying overhead. Enu would even nod and smile to the colorful wild flowers that lined the paths.

On and on the pair walked, deeper into the park. The boy was amazed, even enlightened, by the incredible beauty of the park - once a feared foe, now a fine friend. They cavorted along creeks and jumped over gullies. They crossed old bridges and scrambled under fallen trees. At one point along the trail, they came to an ancient-looking oak tree. The pair climbed up and sat for a while, perched on a limb that gave them an inspiring view of the park.  It was there that Enu shared with his newest friend stories of worldwide travels, experiencing life from the different perspectives of the vast animal and plant kingdoms.

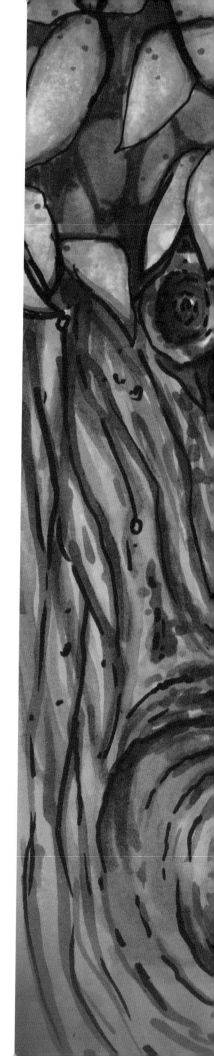

Enu thrilled his companion with stories about flying with the birds high into the heavens and of swimming with the whales who lord over gigantic oceans, whose depths and breadths are immeasurable. Enu described awesome adventures of crawling with the ants on the forest floor of the Amazon, among the roots and into the soil, and of walking with the elephants across vast plains of the Serengeti. Through these extraordinary tales Enu explained to the boy how everything here is connected to everything else.

The boy was absolutely enraptured by Enu's sagas of adventure and travel. He asked the funny little creature endless questions about the world's distinguished and diversified places as well as its mighty mammals and awe-inspiring animals.

At one point, Enu related a tale of soaring along endless miles of coastline as a pelican, much to his admirer's astonishment.

"That is one of my favorite ways to travel! As a pelican I was able to glide just above the ocean surface riding the draft from the waves before they crashed. I could explore the coastline and hunt for fish at the same time. If I got tired I could join other pelicans, who are very welcoming, by the way, and practice flying in a V-formation which made it a little easier." Enu continued, "Sometimes I saw surfers and marveled at how they rode the waves! I even got to practice a little surfing of my own!" Enu chuckled.

"What is it like to fly?" Enu's buddy asked in wonderment.

"It is absolutely amazing!" replied Enu enthusiastically. "But then so is swimming or walking or running or climbing or sitting and watching. It's all amazing. It just depends on your point of view."

The boy was overjoyed listening intently to Enu's enlightening perspectives. He had come to realize that it was not a matter of what he was doing - be it surfing, walking or sitting - but simply a matter of how he looked at it.

*It is all amazing!*
thought the boy.

Finally, Enu told the boy it was time for him to go back and join the hummingbirds. The sun was beginning to set and it was dinnertime for the birds. They made their way back down to the great tree where the two had first met, enjoying the unforgettable sights and enduring sounds along the way. When

they arrived at the tree they said their farewells, but before they parted ways, Enu's new confidante called out, "Wait, one last thing! Of all the places you've been in the world, where's the best place?"

Enu paused for a moment and then replied with a smile, "This place, the one where you are right now, is the very best place!"

After saying this, Enu made a funny little birdcall. A moment later a hummingbird zoomed right past the awed youngster and hovered just above Enu. The boy watched as Enu slowly lifted up his arm and extended his little hand. The hummingbird hovered down slowly and perched gently upon Enu's open palm. As soon as the hummingbird landed, Enu instantly shrunk down in a blur of orange light and transformed back into a hummingbird, complete with a small white streak of feathers on his forehead! The park explorer watched in stunned amazement as Enu slowly rose high up into the air, paused, and then dive-bombed straight down toward his friend and suddenly looped back above his head. Enu made a loud chirping noise and then zoomed off into infinity. The other hummingbird quickly joined Enu and the boy watched as the two birds chased each other into the distance and out of sight.

Enu's pal walked home with a smile on his face. After meeting this fascinating creature, he saw the world with a refreshed perspective and a renewed outlook. The boy knew deep down that the animals, birds, trees, plants, bees, and even the people were all connected, and most importantly, that he was a part of it. As he walked through his neighborhood with a refreshed view on life, the boy understood that the houses and pavement and cars were all just an extension of the great big whale of a planet we call Earth.

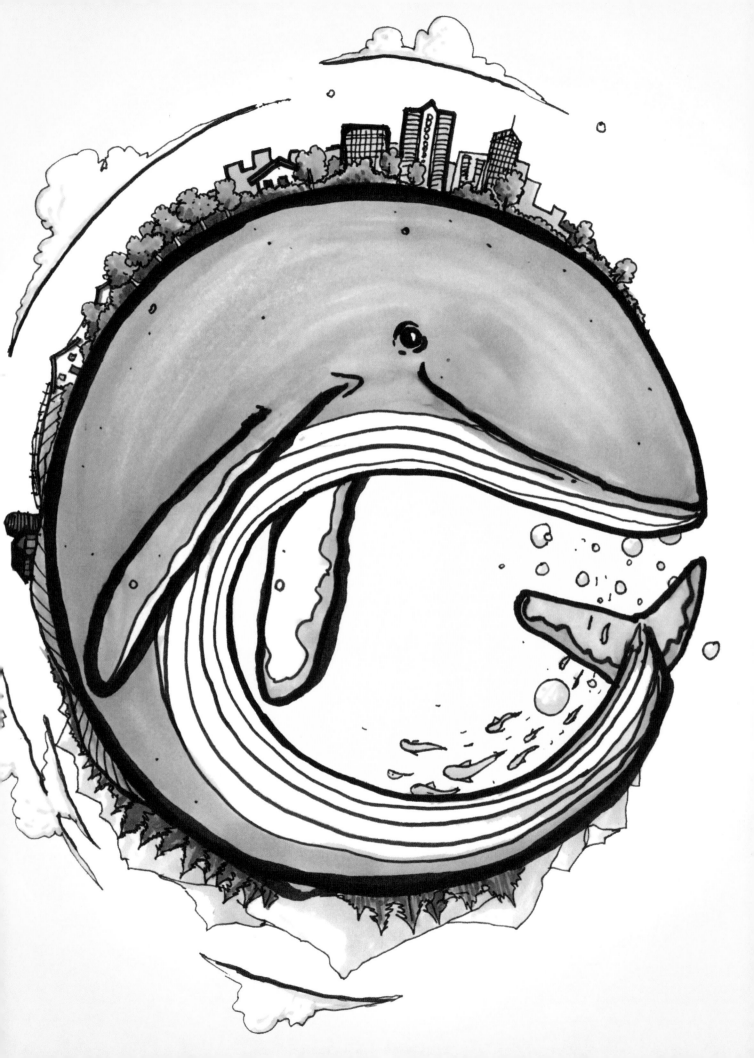

From that point on, the boy no longer complained about moving away from the beach. His summer was full of adventure. He even met some friends in the neighborhood and they began to explore the park together. Sometimes they would spend the entire day at the park running and playing and climbing trees, or just laying in the grass watching the clouds float by.

Other times the boy would visit the park alone and sit in the old oak tree where he had shared cherished words with Enu. The boy would sit and watch and wonder if he would ever see his little orange friend again. But whether he did or he didn't, one thing was for sure.  He never looked at another animal, bird, or bug in the same way because he knew it just might be Enu.

The End

## About the Author

Since he can remember, nature has been a central part of Sebastian's life. He was fortunate to grow up in the beach community of La Jolla, California and spent his childhood in the ocean. Later, he was able to travel extensively and experience many of the world's great surf spots as a professional bodyboarder. Through his travel, Sebastian developed a deep love and appreciation for our natural world, and at the same time was drawn to the practice of yoga. Sebastian currently lives in San Diego, California where he leads individuals and small groups on guided surf/nature/yoga adventures around Southern California and abroad, combining yoga with activities like hiking, surfing, and stand-up paddling as a unique method of self-discovery and a wonderful way to reconnect with nature. He is the founder of Nature Unplugged, a company aimed at promoting healthier, happier, and more balanced living through connecting with nature.

## About the Illustrator

A native of San Diego, California, Blaze Syka was drawn to art at a young age. His interest in art and nature was further fueled by his passion for surfing and the ocean. He became an ocean lifeguard at age 15 in Del Mar, California. The years guarding and surfing inspired Blaze to become an ocean-minded individual, a concept he depicts and expresses in many of his pieces. Blaze graduated from Cal Poly San Luis Obispo in 2012 and currently lives in Morro Bay on California's Central Coast where he continues to chase his passions in art, nature, and the ocean.

Made in the USA
Columbia, SC
22 December 2017